Legend of the Christmas Tree

Barbara Starr Crank

Illustrations by Blueberry Illustrations

ISBN: 978-0-9994104-0-0

A portion of the proceeds from *Legend of the Christmas Tree* will be donated to the Christian Farm Retreat, a non-profit corporation formed to convert 120 acres of farm land into a family friendly environment of outdoor recreation as well as faith based and living educational opportunities.

In addition, there could be a fundraising opportunity for your group or organization. Through the Christian Farm Retreat, funds can be generated by schools, churches, missions, ministries, sports groups, nonprofits, and faith based organizations that participate in the *Legend of the Christmas Tree* Fundraiser.

If you would like to take advantage of the *Legend of the Christmas Tree* Fundraiser contact CFR for information on how you can get started.

Phone: 937-205-4616
Email: info@christianfarmretreat.com
Message via the Christian Farm Retreat website:
www.christianfarmretreat.com

In loving memory of my father, Charles
Madden. Each Christmas Eve he enjoyed gathering
all the children around the Christmas tree to share
with them the importance of the evergreen to the
life of animals. He would say that the evergreen
is the perfect decoration to bring into our homes
as we celebrate the birth of Christ because the
reason Jesus came was to offer us life, in a sense,
like the evergreen offers life to the animals. My
father's greatest passions in life were preaching and
fishing. Since I don't imagine there is a high demand
for preachers in Heaven, this is for the fisherman
casting a line into the crystal river and for all the
children here that he would love for us to gather
around the Christmas tree to tell them about Jesus.

I love you, Dad, and may *Legend of the Christmas
Tree* help to carry on your tradition of gathering
the children around the Christmas tree.

Many years ago, on a cold, cold Christmas Eve morning, Golden Eagle looked to see if anything in the kingdom stirred. A blanket of snow covered the ground, and the bare trees shimmered in their coats of thick ice, under a timid sun. If this bitterness continued, soon all the creatures in the forest would die without food and warmth.

Golden Eagle shivered in the frigid cold. He stretched his wings, shook them, and fluffed his feathers as he settled down on the frozen bough. His chest tightened as he slowly turned his head from side to side and surveyed the area for Songbird. But he found no movement in the forest.

Golden Eagle struck a limb with his sharp beak and a loud crack sounded as the ice split. Chips flew in all directions as he freed the branch from ice. The deliciously sweet smell of sassafras soon filled the air. Spreading his massive wings, he lifted into the dawn, carrying the cleaned branch in his talons for Songbird and the others to eat. His wings were heavy as he flapped them. He slowed, and a mist formed over his eyes. He too needed warmth and nourishment. Finally, he spotted Songbird and Rabbit in the clearing and swooped down to give them the branch.

A sudden sharp pain shot through Golden Eagle's back as Black Vulture grabbed onto him with his talons. Black Vulture hissed as he dug deep into Golden Eagle's back and beat at him with a hard flapping of his wings. Golden Eagle dropped the branch and turned his powerful talons toward Black Vulture. Black Vulture cowered, disappearing into the clouds.

Gliding through the air, Golden Eagle searched for Black Vulture, his shoulder hurt from the attack. He heard the clamor of bickering and quarreling arising from the animals in the forest. Golden Eagle flapped his wings to thrust into flight but one of his wings drooped sending stings into his body and then he felt himself plummeting.

Golden Eagle crashed into the clearing. Lying on the ground, he could see Black Vulture again circling in the sky. Songbird and Rabbit rushed to help him as the other forest animals gathered into the clearing.

Golden Eagle spread his great wings and tried to lift into the air but his injured wing was too weak. Golden Eagle looked around at the famished forest animals and he saw fear in their eyes. His heart was heavy for them. They were unprepared to face the harsh winter trials, and most probably would not endure until spring.

Peace and joy was far from the forest as most of the animals looked out only for themselves. Their hungry bellies and selfish thoughts caused arguments to arise as they foraged through the frozen forest searching for food.

Golden Eagle gazed into the heavens and sighed. He yearned to dance in the sky one more time before death came upon him. Songbird pushed in under his wing and snuggled close to his breast as they watched Black Vulture circle the area. Songbird tenderly sang about a special place she'd envisioned. "There is a place to cherish where life lives on and does not perish."

Rabbit heard Songbird's song and hopped into the clearing. "Is it true about this place, or is it just a dream?"

Bunny ears perked up across the dell, as stories grew of the special place that offered life instead of the deadly chill.

Chattering squirrels now echoed the tale, as they dreamed of delicious things and trees of green.

"Where is this place that offers warmth, nourishment and protection to weary hungry wanderers?" the deep voice of Buck asked as he led his starving family across the clearing.

The shrieking chant of Black Vulture then rang out as he dove into their midst. "There is no such place. There is only here."

Golden Eagle helplessly watched as Black Vulture swooped down over a family of mice scurrying away in fear.

"There is only this place and it belongs to me. You must stay here and live in fear." Black Vulture shrieked a wicked laugh as he flew into the sky. He circled round and round again, peering to the ground, and sending warning shrieks to anyone who dared to speak of the special place offering the gift of life.

But the rising voice of hope could not be hushed, and animals from all around chattered of the special place. Songbird sang, "I know it's real, it's not a dream. God, help me find the way." And then she flew out from them to look for the special place.

Songbird returned late that afternoon hungry, frozen, and weary without finding the way. The sadness in her eyes was almost more than Golden Eagle could bear. Hopelessness overcame the animals as Black Vulture's shadow continually passed over the land.

Golden Eagle gathered Songbird and his tiny furry friends under his wings as the sun went down that Christmas Eve. He gave comfort and warmth as best he could with the fading heat of his body.

Golden Eagle surveyed the sky in awe as his little friends slept under the shelter of his wings. The brilliance of an eastern star arose and shone a light like no star he'd ever seen. Golden Eagle roused Songbird and motioned toward the star. With an excited peep, she immediately flew into the light and soon returned chirping a brand new song. "I've seen it! It's true! There's a tree that's forever green. It offers everything that we might have life."

Excitement grew and hope swelled in the hearts of the furry and feathered companions as Songbird sang the sweet melody over and over again.

And so it was that their journey to the special
place began as all who believed followed
the bright eastern star into the night.

It was nearly daybreak on Christmas morning when Black Vulture plunged into their midst to turn them back. With wings spread and ready to fight, Golden Eagle mustered up his loudest call to challenge Black Vulture. But Black Vulture only ignored the challenge and swiftly snatched Rabbit up instead. Screeching his wicked evil laugh, he circled around about dangling Rabbit for all to see.

Songbird flew up and mobbed Black Vulture, pecking at his neck and wings relentlessly, trying to make him let Rabbit go. And Black Vulture did. He dropped Rabbit in midair and immediately did a barrel roll, flashing his angry talons at Songbird.

Golden Eagle whispered a prayer, "Through your strength, God, let me do this." And then his swiftness lifted him gracefully into the air, where he caught Rabbit and glided him safely to the ground. Golden Eagle rocketed back into the sky, flapping with deep wing-beats until he was soaring far above Black Vulture and Songbird. With wings tight and partly closed against his body, Golden Eagle dove hard and fast toward Black Vulture. Moving his claws forward as he neared the evil predator, he reached out and with one quick hit, he snatched Black Vulture up and flew him far away from Songbird and the other forest animals.

Golden Eagle returned and then he and Songbird led the way as they continued to follow the brilliance of the star. It led them to a special place where an enormous evergreen stood in the middle of the white wonderland. It was stunning, with thick, dark green branches covered in wonderfully scrumptious pinecones filled with mouthwatering seeds. Attending this magnificent tree was a beautiful angel dressed in white who said, "Christmas travelers, welcome to the tree of life that God has provided to all who will come, believing and receiving freely of His gift."

Golden Eagle graced the heavens with his most spectacular sky dance that Christmas morning and then gracefully he flew into the clouds of Heaven where God looked down to see Songbird nestled warmly in the arms of Evergreen. The squirrels were cozy in the branches with their bellies filled with seeds. Rabbit had burrowed deep under Evergreen and made a comfortable home for all the little bunnies. Buck and his family were nearby in a bed of fallen needles, nibbling sweet pinecones. In the protective arms of Evergreen, it was a very merry Christmas for Songbird and the forest animals.

And then all of Heaven heard Songbird burst into song, "O Christmas Tree! O Christmas Tree! Thy leaves are so unchanging; Not only green when summer's here, But also when 'tis cold and drear."

As Songbird sang, birds hung brightly colored feathers on Evergreen. Squirrels gathered berries and strung them along its branches. The deer family laid gifts of moss and ferns around the base of the tree. Rabbit retrieved a golden feather that had fallen from Golden Eagle and gave it to the mice to place upon the tree. All the forest animals gathered around the adorned Evergreen and joined with Songbird in chorus to celebrate Christmas, the birth of baby Jesus.

"O Christmas Tree! O Christmas Tree!
How richly God has decked thee!
Thou bidst us true and faithful be,
And trust in God unchangingly.
O Christmas Tree! O Christmas Tree!
How richly God has decked thee!"

God was very pleased, and told the angel to place the eastern star upon that very first Christmas tree.

Our legend of the first Christmas tree ends here, but the evergreen tree will always remind us that God is creator of all things and the giver of life. We bring the evergreen into our homes once a year and adorn it with beautiful things to give glory and praise to Jesus Christ our Savior. We place the star on top of the tree to remind us that the light comes from God in Heaven to show the way for the lost and endangered that none should perish but all could have everlasting life.

Barbara Starr Crank has been teaching and serving children through leadership in children's and youth programs for over thirty years. Working alongside her husband, Keith, in pastoring and church planting, she recognizes that spiritual growth requires knowledge of biblical truth and values in both adults and children alike. Her desire is to encourage the development of faith in children and to emphasize the importance of faith based activities and traditions in the home.

Keith and Starr have two adult children and three beautiful grandchildren. They enjoy life on a rural farm growing organic blueberries and watching their grandchildren parade around the blueberry bushes using their imaginations to be whatever it is they want to be on any given day. She is mostly known as Meemee to children, but will gladly answer to Barbara, Barbara Starr, or simply Starr.

Connect with her on Facebook @StarrCrank or on her website at **www.starrcrank.com**.